'Scotty'

'John Grey'

'Chipper'

Fluffy

'Ol' Salty'

'Stubbs'

'Edgar Bone'

Fluffy

Scourge
of the Sea

For Sarah, Natalie, Rosamarie, Esther, and Launa, who have always
appreciated the power of "cute" and the awesome responsibility it entails.
—T. B.

To Maggie
—M. C.

"The Jolly Rover"

Fluffy

Scourge
of the Sea

Teresa Bateman   *Illustrated by Michael Chesworth*

Charlesbridge

He was just a pampered poodle
Sailing seaward on his yacht,
When a pirate ship approached
And in a moment he was caught.

Scurvy pooches took him prisoner.
They hauled that dog aboard.
At the sight of him the pirates snickered,
Then the pirates roared.

"Cute outfit," said the pirate chief,
"And it would be a shame
To get that sweet bow mussied up.
Now, tell us all your name!"

The poor dog looked into their eyes.
He knew what they would say.
His name was on his collar—
They would find out anyway.

So, being a resourceful pooch,
He growled most savagely.
"I'm Fluffy," said that poodle.
"Fluffy—Scourge of All the Sea!"

The pirates looked quite doubtful,
As well the pirates ought.
A "scourge" should not wear pretty bows,
Nor sail upon a yacht.

"I've never heard of you."
The pirate captain gave a sneer.
"And I know every rascal
Who has been a privateer!"

Bold Fluffy strutted on the deck
With eyes as cold as lead.
"If you knew who I am," he said,
"You'd wish that you were dead."

The poodle looked so powerful
He made the pirates quail.
Despite the bow, he looked a buccaneer
From nose to tail.

"Then prove it," said the pirate chief.
He tossed the dog a sword.
"Let's have a little fun before
We throw you overboard."

But Fluffy'd gone to fencing school.
"En garde!" that poodle cried.
And he chased the pirate captain
As he ran from side to side.

While the captain tried to catch his breath,
The poodle paused in thought.
"Perhaps," considered Fluffy,
"I deserve more than a yacht!"

He looked that pirate in the eye.
A grim smile curled his lip.
"I don't think you deserve the job
Of captaining this ship!

"Perhaps a few more contests
Will reveal which dog will do.
First off, I am appalled to see
This hangdog, scrawny crew."

He whipped them up a meal supreme.
The mutts began to drool.
The pirate captain made a vat
Of lumpy oatmeal gruel.

The crew compared their servings.
It was clear who'd won the show.
If this was Fluffy's pirate fare,
Who cared about a bow?

The captain heard their murmurs,
And he started to feel scared.
"I challenge you to sing a pirate song!"
He quickly dared.

He bellowed out a ballad
About Doggy Jones below,
Of pilfered bones and creaky masts,
And dead dogs' chests—"Yo ho!"

But Fluffy sang a song of hope,
Of love that lasts the years,
Of winds that take you home again. . . .
The crew's eyes filled with tears.

The crew compared the singing,
And their votes were all the same.
If this was Fluffy's pirate song,
Who cared about a name?

The captain's desperation flared.
He glanced at Fluffy's yacht.
"He's not a buccaneer!" he cried.
"Let's find out what he's got!"

They searched his boat most carefully
And found, to their surprise,
Expensive bags of kibble,
Rubber bones, and liver pies.

The captain cocked a furry brow,
But Fluffy kept his head.
"I said I was a pirate. That's my loot,"
The poodle said.

The mongrel crew was quite impressed.
They gave their chief a hiss.
In all their years of pirating
They'd not seen loot like this.

"I vote we change our captain,"
Said an eye-patched old bowwow.
"If that's the type of loot he has,
I'll follow Fluffy now."

The captain backed across the deck,
Fainthearted and weak-kneed.
"It's mutiny!" the captain cried,
And all of them agreed.

They set him on the open sea
With hardtack and a raft.
"Hurrah for Captain Fluffy!" they all cried.
The poodle laughed.

"My first act as your captain,"
Fluffy told them with a grin,
"Is to show you there's a better way
Than piracy to win.

"No need to rob and steal to get
A yacht, good food, and loot.
There's a world of riches waiting
For a dog who's just plain cute."

They cleaned the ship,
Shampooed their fur,
Shined up their buckled shoes.
They put on fluffy bows and then
They went out for a cruise.

And, sure enough, at every port,
Folks flocked with oohs and aahs
To hand them bones and liver pies,
And shake their perfumed paws.

"How sweet!" old ladies murmured.
"See the puppy buccaneers?"
"Aren't they cute?" the children giggled
As they scratched the pirates' ears.

Their holds were full, their bellies, too—
Their lives were now carefree.
And they owed it all to Fluffy,
Fluffy—Scourge of All the Sea!

Published by Charlesbridge
85 Main Street
Watertown, MA 02472
(617) 926-0329
www.charlesbridge.com

Library of Congress Cataloging-in-Publication Data
Bateman, Teresa.
Fluffy, Scourge of the Sea / Teresa Bateman ; illustrated by Michael Chesworth.
p.   cm.
When Fluffy, a pampered poodle, is captured by canine pirates, he uses
his wiles to convince them that he is in reality the "Scourge of all the Sea."
ISBN 1-58089-099-7 (reinforced for library use)
[1. Poodles—Fiction. 2. Dogs—Fiction. 3. Pirates—Fiction. 4. Stories in rhyme.] I. Chesworth, Michael, ill. II. Title.
PZ8.3.B314Fl 2005
[E]—dc22   2004003300

Printed in China
(hc) 10 9 8 7 6 5 4 3 2 1

Illustrations done in watercolor with colored pencil on Fabriano 140 lbs. hot press watercolor paper
Display type and text type set in Allegheny and Truesdell
Color separated, printed, and bound by R.R. Donnelley
Production supervision by Brian G. Walker
Designed by Diane M. Earley

'Shep'

'Moody'

'Lil' Jack'

The Captain

'the Jolly Rover'

'Lucky'

'Wolfie'